This is Pongo.

Pongo is a very playful gorilla.

He lives in the mountains in Africa.

Pongo wants to be as brave
and clever as his dad.

He wants a big silver chest
to thump!

But will Pongo ever learn
to grow up?

Also by Jill Tomlinson

Jill Tomlinson

The Gorilla Who Wanted to Grow Up

Pictures by **Paul Howard**

EGMONT

To Rolfe, my beloved gorilla,

and the rest of the troop;

and, of course, DH.

EGMONT
We bring stories to life

First published in Great Britain 1977 by Methuen Children's Books Ltd
Published in this edition 2014 by Egmont UK Limited
The Yellow Building, 1 Nicholas Road, London W11 4AN

Text copyright © 1977 The Estate of Jill Tomlinson
Cover and illustrations copyright © 2004 Paul Howard

The moral rights of the illustrator have been asserted

ISBN 978 1 4052 7195 0

www.egmont.co.uk

A CIP catalogue record for this title is available from the British Library

Typeset by Avon DataSet Ltd, Bidford on Avon, Warwickshire
Printed and bound in Great Britain by the CPI Group

42446/16

Contents

Pongo

Pongo was a young gorilla. He lived in the mountains of Africa. He had long glossy black hair and a black shiny nose. His arms were long and he walked on the knuckles of his hands on all fours. He could stand upright like a man but he didn't walk very far or very often like this.

Pongo lived in a troop of gorillas and his father was the leader. Pongo called him Da but the other gorillas called him the Big Boss. Da looked quite different from Pongo, apart from being much bigger. There were white hairs all over his back mixed with the black ones, so his back looked silver. Pongo's troop passed other

troops sometimes and the leader always had a silver back like Da. Pongo often wondered why.

When Pongo was younger he lived with his mother but now that he was growing up he spent much more time with Da. Sometimes he leaned against him for his afternoon nap.

One day Pongo felt Da stirring and knew that he could ask him some questions. 'Da,' he said, 'will I have a silver back like you?'

'Yes, when you're a big chap like me,' said Da.

'When will that be?' Pongo asked.

'Oh, when you're ten or eleven, I think.'

'How old am I now?' Pongo asked.

'I don't really know,' Da said. 'I've forgotten. But you're tall already so I don't think it can be very long before you have a silver back.'

'Will I get a big chest like you?' Pongo asked. 'And be able to thump it? I've always wanted to do that.'

'Yes, you will,' da said, 'but not just yet. You'll have to wait a little while. When you're grown up you'll be in charge of the troop yourself.'

'A troop of my own?' Pongo said. 'with my own wives and children?'

'That's it,' Da said. 'Now I want to sleep some more. Go and play with your friends.'

Pongo went off to play with the other young gorillas. They always had a good game when the grown-ups were sleeping. There were lots of things to do in the rain forest where they lived. They could climb up and down the trees and swing on the creepers that hung from the trees. They could chase each other and fight – but very gently because gorillas never hurt each other. When one of them had had enough he crouched down and held one of his arms across the back of his neck. This always stopped the fight.

Pongo was sitting under a tree wondering what to do when something hurled itself at him.

'You lazy lump,' it cried. The something was Zambi, Pongo's best friend.

'I'm not lazy,' Pongo said. 'I was just deciding what to do.'

'Well you're a jolly slow decider,' Zambi said. 'I've decided I'm going to roll you over that cliff.'

'What cliff?' Pongo asked. 'That miserable little bank over there?'

They began wrestling on the top of the bank. They enjoyed fighting because they

were almost exactly the same size. Zambi
suddenly rolled over and Pongo was jerked
over the bank. It was in fact a slippery slope.
It was great fun sliding down.

'Zambi!' Pongo called. 'Come and join
me. This is great fun.'

Zambi was already just behind him.

'There, you see what a good friend
I am,' he said. 'This is a lovely
place for a game.'

It was, too. It was difficult getting back up again but they soon found some bushes and creepers to pull themselves up with. They went on playing there until they were tired. Sitting at the bottom Zambi said, 'We must tell the others about this.'

'Not yet,' Pongo said. 'I've been talking to Da and I want to tell you what he told me.' And that's what he did.

'So you want a silver back?' Zambi said. 'Don't you want to play games any more? The Boss doesn't play games very much.'

'Well, he can't,' Pongo said. 'His job is too look after us all. I suppose when I have a silver back I'll be too busy to play games. No, you're right. I'll just enjoy being what I am for the moment.'

He did, too. He got Zambi to climb on to

a rock and then tried to push him off it. This was a favourite game of theirs. I'm the King of the Castle. Then they noticed the Big Boss getting up and reaching round him for food. It was eating time. They stopped playing and began to do the same themselves. This was a good part of the forest because there was food everywhere. Gorillas eat nettles and leaves of all kinds and the pulp out of the stems of plants; even bark off trees. And in this part of the forest they hardly had to move to find more food. They were surrounded by it and they ate and ate until they could eat no more.

After he'd finished eating, the Big Boss began to make himself a nest. That only meant picking up a few bundles of leaves and putting them round him. He laid down to go to sleep then. All the other gorillas copied him.

It was sleeping time. That was what his job was, to show everybody what to do and when to do it. The Big Boss himself always slept on the ground now because he was too big and heavy. But Pongo was still light enough to sleep up a tree. He made a nest with his mother. She had a surprise for him tonight.

'You won't be able to sleep with me much longer, Pongo,' she said. 'You're going to have to sleep on the ground like Da.'

'I know I'm getting bigger,' Pongo said, 'but can't we make a stronger nest?'

'Not strong enough for three,' Ma said.

'Three?' Pongo said. 'You mean we're going to have another baby?'

'That's right,' Ma said.

'When?' Pongo asked.

'Oh, I don't know that, but quite soon,'

Ma said. 'And you can help me look after it.'

'You've got Da,' Pongo said.

'But Da's very busy. I think I shall need you sometimes,' Ma said. 'But come on, let's go to sleep now. goodnight, Pongo.'

'Goodnight, Ma,' Pongo said.

So they went to sleep in their nest and Da went to sleep at the bottom of the tree.

Man

The next morning the sun was shining. The Big Boss was feeling lazy and had breakfast in bed. That wasn't difficult. All he had to do was reach out and pick some celery. Pongo was just getting ready to climb down the tree and join him when Da roared, and that was quite a noise. He stood up on his hind legs and stuck out his great chest and threw bits of celery in the air. Then he began to thump ths palms of his hands on his chest. It made a sound like a war-drum echoing through the forest, making all the gorillas sit up and listen.

'Don't move,' Pongo's mother said. 'That means danger.'

'Danger?' Pongo said. 'What danger? You told me we've only got one enemy. Man.'

'Yes,' his mother said. 'What do you think that is over there?'

Then Pongo saw the man. He was standing under a tree looking at them.

'It's all right, Ma,' said Pongo. 'He hasn't got a gun or a spear.'

'No, he hasn't, has he?' Ma said. 'But let's wait and see what Da decides.'

Da charged at the man, throwing up leaves as he went. The man didn't move. He seemed to be enjoying the war dance.

Da stopped and stared at the man for a moment and then went back to his nest and went on eating.

Ma laughed. 'That man's seen gorillas before,' she said. 'Men usually run away when they see Da charging like that. But he just stood still. Da's eating now, so he doesn't think the man is dangerous. Come on, we'll go and have our breakfast too.'

So Pongo and his mother climbed down the tree and began eating. They stayed near Da though. The rest of the gorillas stayed near the Big Boss too. Although he was waiting, the Big Boss kept an eye on the man.

Zambi came over to Pongo. 'Why is that man watching us like that?' he said. 'Perhaps he thinks we're dangerous, and that's why he's keeping a little way away.'

'No,' Pongo said. 'He's not afraid of us because he didn't move when Da charged him.'

They went on eating like Da. But when they were full Zambi said to Pongo: 'He's still watching us, that man. Let's go and watch him.'

They crept a bit closer to him, keeping well hidden behind a thicket.

'Look,' whispered Zambi. 'He's pulling something out of that bag. Perhaps it's a gun.'

'I don't think you eat guns,' Pongo said. 'and that's what he's doing. Anyway, I don't think guns are little white things like that.'

It was just a sandwich.

'I'd like to try one of those things,' said Zambi.

'Gorillas don't pinch each others food,' Pongo said. 'So we don't pinch man's food either.'

Just then the man reached into his bag and pulled something else out.

'Look, it's a banana,' Pongo said. 'He's peeling it and eating it.'

'Ugh! Doesn't he know that the only nice part of the banana tree is the pulp out of the stem.'

They went back and told Da about this funny man.

'I don't think he's very dangerous,' Pongo said. 'But it's fun watching him.'

'Well, you do that,' said Da. 'Watch him. You have to learn about man. Know your enemy is a good rule.'

'He's not an enemy,' Pongo said.

'No, I don't think he is,' Da said. 'And that makes it easier to watch him safely. So you go and learn about him.'

'I've just learned something,' said Zambi. 'From here. Look. He's taller than Da.'

They all looked at him.

'He's as thin as a creeper, though,' said Pongo. 'Da must be ten times as wide as he is.'

'Well, he's not a creeper, so don't try to climb him,' said Da. 'I don't think he could take your weight. He's quite old; look at his hair.'

They looked.

'It's white,' Pongo said. 'And he has lines on his face just like a very old gorilla.'

'Yes, he's old,' Da said. 'Only old men have white hair. So you be gentle with him.'

'I don't know,' Zambi said to Pongo. 'Your Da's getting old too. Now we've got to be gentle with our enemies.'

'He's not an enemy,' Pongo said. 'Da knows what he's doing. You get wiser as you 'get older, usually.'

'Oh, of course, you'd know that,' Zambi said. 'Well, a wise old man like you . . .'

'Someone round here,' interrupted Pongo, 'seems to be asking for a fight.' And that's what they had, till they decided to go on eating as usual.

Later Da began to make his nest. Pongo began to make one near Zambi.

'I thought you slept up the tree with your mother?' Zambi said.

'No, I'm getting too heavy,' Pongo said. 'May I stay near you?'

'Yes,' Zambi said. 'It will be nice to have company.'

'Is the man making a nest?' Pongo said.

'I don't expect so,' said Zambi. 'Men don't like to make nests near fierce gorillas like me!' And, sure enough, when they sat in their nests afterwards the man had gone.

Whoopsie

The next morning after breakfast Pongo set
out to see if he could find the man. Da had
told him to look for a big nest made of tree
trunks. Pongo found it and he was amazed.
This wasn't like one of their nests because it
had a sort of top to it. That man wasn't
going to get wet when it rained! There didn't
seem to be anyone near the nest so Pongo
looked through a hole in the side of it. He was

so surprised at what he saw that he rushed straight back to Da to tell him about it.

'That man,' he said. 'He was taking the fur off his face with a sort of scratcher thing. I think he must have done his chest and arms as well, because he was quite bare.'

Da laughed. 'Men are bare,' he said. 'That's why they put coverings on to keep warm. they haven't got nice warm coats like us. Oh look, here he comes now. Shall I do a war dance, do you think?'

'No,' Pongo said. 'You know he's safe to have around.'

'Well, keep an eye on him for me, Pongo,' Da said. 'I want to get on with my breakfast. But I don't think he's going to be any trouble.'

Pongo didn't watch the man very much. He was hungry and wanted to get on with his breakfast. Gorillas need to eat an awful lot, because they only eat plants and things and they need a lot to make them strong. Pongo was so busy eating he forgot all about the man.

Then something began to puzzle him. Usually Da took them a little way away from where they had eaten a day before, but he hadn't today. There was plenty of food so they didn't really need to move, but it was puzzling.

They found out the reason at rest-time. It was a very nice reason. Ma had been having her baby. Pongo saw his mother coming towards Da with something in her arms. Something with bare arms which were hanging round her neck.

'Look!' Pongo said to Zambi. 'Look!'

Ma handed the little bare baby to Da

and he stroked it and then handed it back.

'She's lovely,' he said. 'Now you go and sit in the shade.'

'I've got a sister,' Pongo said. 'A baby sister. I wonder what we're going to call her. I'll go and ask Da.'

'We haven't decided yet,' said Da. 'I expect we will later on.'

Pongo and Zambi were watching Ma with the baby and Zambi said to Pongo, 'I thought babies rode on their mother's backs.'

'Not very new babies,' Pongo said. 'They're not strong enough to hang on. Ma will carry her until she's strong enough.'

'You seem to know an awful lot,' Zambi said. 'Where did you find that out?'

'We see other troops going past,' Pongo said.

'I don't take much notice of other troops,' Zambi said.

'No, you're too busy eating,' said Pongo. 'That makes me wonder. How is Ma going to eat with her arms full of baby? Perhaps I'd better feed her.'

He went and asked Da.

'No, that's all right, son,' he said. 'She'll hold the baby with one arm and eat with the other one. She's not as greedy as you; she doesn't need to stuff her food in with both hands. She'll manage.'

So they went on eating and later on had a rest in the sun. Gorillas love the sun so when there is any they enjoy it. But Zambi had a surprise; the man was sunbathing too.

'Look,' he said to Pongo. 'Our man. He's got a spotted rump. He's taken off his arm coverings and his leg coverings and he's lying in the sun like us.'

Pongo looked lazily over at the man. 'Yes, you're right. He has a spotted rump like a leopard and he likes the sun like us. That's something we've learned about man.'

Of course, man was wearing his swimming trunks but the gorillas didn't know that.

Nothing much happened for the rest of that day and it was too hot to move. At bedtime Pongo made a nest for his mother. He chose a tree with a fork very low down. Pongo began to bend the branches in all round the fork and this made a very good nest. He was growing up and knew what he was doing. But not quite. He came down the tree to Da.

'Da,' he said, 'how will Ma get the baby

into the nest? She can't climb up a tree holding a baby.'

'You go and fetch her and I'll show you,' Da said.

So Pongo fetched his mother and sister. He understood as soon as he got back to the tree. Da was tall and he could reach the nest easily.

'Can I hold my sister while you climb up to the nest I've made you?' Pongo said.

'Yes, of course you can,' Ma said. 'Here you are.'

'Isn't she tiny?' Pongo said to Da, holding his little sister against his chest.

'She's really small.'

'She'll grow up very quickly,' said Da. 'You'll see.'

Ma called down from the nest. 'Ready.'

Pongo stood under the tree. 'Da,' he said, 'I'm tall enough to hand her up myself.'

'I had a feeling you might be,' he said. 'All right, you give her to Ma.'

Pongo gave his little sister one last hug and then he said, 'Now, up you go. One, two, three, whoopsie,' and handed her up to Ma.

'Whoopsie,' Da said. 'That's a nice name. shall we call her Whoopsie, Ma?'

'Yes,' she said, and holding Whoopsie to her she said, 'There, your brother's named you. Pongo says you're to be called Whoopsie.'

While they were making their own nests Pongo said to Da, 'Whoopsie is tiny and she's so bare, she's as bare as that man.'

Da laughed. 'She won't be for long,' he said. 'She'll have a coat like yours in a week or two. You'll see.'

The Job

Da was quite right about Whoopsie. She was soon covered with black hair and not bare any more. She was soon riding on her mother's back, too. Then one day Pongo saw Ma with no baby on her back. Where was Whoopsie? Pongo rushed over and then he saw that Whoopsie was happily lying on the ground while her mother was eating.

'Is she safe down there?' Pongo asked Ma.

'Of course she is,' Ma said. 'She'll be crawling before long. But she can't learn to do that on my back. She's got to be on the ground.'

Pongo understood, but he ate near them for a bit because he wanted to be quite sure that Whoopsie was safe. He was just pulling up a fern to take a bite when he felt a hand on his shoulder. He looked round to find Da.

'You're a good lad, Pongo,' he said. 'But you know it's just possible that Ma knows what she's doing. Whoopsie isn't her first baby.'

'I just wanted to be sure they were safe,' Pongo said. 'And I didn't know you were near.'

'I wasn't,' Da said. 'But I think this is a good moment for me to ask you something that I've been meaning to ask you for a little while now.'

'Yes?' Pongo said, putting down his fern.

'Well, it's like this,' Da said. 'You're getting to be a big chap now; you've begun to shoot.'

'Shoot?' Pongo said. 'What does that mean? I haven't got a gun.'

'No, you're growing very much taller, which means that you're growing up. Now this is what I want to ask you. You and Zambi are the two oldest of the youngsters and I need you to help me. Lately we've been staying round the same bit of forest because it's very good here, but sometimes we make a sort of procession to move along a path to a new place. Now I need someone I can trust at the very back, a sentinel.'

'A what?' asked Pongo.

'A rear guard. Someone who can make sure that it's safe at the back of the procession. Zambi can help and you can work together. It's very important. I'll go at the front leading

the procession; then there's Ma and Whoopsie
and all the females and the youngsters. I must
be sure that the back is safe. You must warn
me if anything dangerous comes near. That
means you must roar and bang your chest.
Or perhaps you had better bang the stump
of a tree, because you haven't got a very big
chest yet. Anyway, we shan't be moving for
a day or two so you and Zambi can practise.
Will you do this for me?'

'Oh, yes,' Pongo said. 'My chest seems
bigger already. I feel much more grown up
having a real job to do.'

'Well, go and tell Zambi about it,' Da said.
'I'll look after Ma and Whoopsie for you.'

Pongo rushed off to find Zambi, banging his
chest hard all the way. Zambi ran to meet him.

'What's the matter?' he said. 'Danger?'

Pongo laughed. 'No, I'm just practising,' he said. 'We've got a job, you and I.' And he told Zambi all about it.

For the next few days all the other gorillas spent a lot of time huddling round the Big Boss because Pongo and Zambi were roaring and thumping trees and their chests. Da explained to the rest of the gorillas that Pongo and Zambi were only practising, but some of them were still a bit frightened very time they started. And that was often, because Pongo and Zambi were practising whenever they weren't eating or sleeping. Pongo soon had a great big roar, but Zambi hadn't.

'Well, I'm younger than you,' he said to Pongo.

'Yes,' Pongo said. 'And you're good at tree-banging. With two of us at it we can warn Da. That's what matters.'

One day Da came up and inspected them.

'Well, I think you can stop practising now,' he said. 'Some of the old girls are in a perpetual state of fright.'

'There's nothing for them to be afraid of, anyway,' Pongo said. 'We haven't seen a thing.'

'No, it's pretty safe up here in the mountains,' Da said, 'though sometimes you get men with spears and things like that. Very, very occasionally you find a leopard, but usually they keep well away from us. A chap like me can tear a leopard in half and they know it.'

'What about the creeper,' Zambi said. 'Do we have to roar for him?' the creeper was the name they used for the man because he was so thin.

Da laughed. 'No,' he said. 'He seems to be one of the troop now; he's always with us. I think he'd better be in front of you so you can keep him safe. A leopard might go for him. Well now you can go and play. You're off duty. But I'll tell you when I need you.'

So that's how it was. A few days later Da took them along a path to a new place and he asked Pongo and Zambi to bring up the rear of the troop. The man didn't seem a bit surprised to find Pongo and Zambi behind him when he had tacked on to the back of the troop.

There was only one awkward moment that morning. Another troop passed them going the other way. The other leader and Da exchanged nods and that was all right. But when the other leader saw the man he stopped. He was just beginning to pull up some leaves to throw into the air before he roared when, to Pongo's amazement, the man nodded his head from side to side. That is the gorilla sign for 'we mean no harm'. So Pongo nodded as well, and Zambi did too. Then, the leader of the other troop went on past them.

'Where did you learn to do that?' Zambi asked Pongo.

'Watching other troops,' Pongo said. 'and that's where the man learned it too, I suppose. I told you he must have been with gorillas before. He's a clever old chap.'

When they reached the place where Da had been leading them soon afterwards, they found it was a field full of blackberries. They sat around stuffing their mouths with fruit until they could eat no more. Then they all fell asleep.

They made their nests that night in the forest near to the field. There wasn't a black-berry left by the time they had finished.

Fun and games

Life went on as usual in their new surroundings.
But one day Pongo had a surprise. He was
having a little snooze with all the others when
he felt something tugging at him. He looked
down sleepily and then his eyes nearly popped
out. It was Whoopsie. Where had she come
from? Ma was some way away.

'What are you doing here?' Pongo asked.

'Pongo,' she said, and tugged at him again.

She wanted him to play with her. Whoopsie had been growing up and she could crawl now. That's how she had reached Pongo. Ma was a very long way away. Well, Pongo played with her. It was quite clear that that's what Whoopsie thought brothers were for. He rolled her over and over. She liked that. And he threw her up and down and caught her.

'Now, come on, climb on my back and I'll give you a ride back to Ma. She'll be wondering where you are,' Pongo said after a while.

Whoopsie didn't understand straight away but he lay on his tummy and of course she climbed onto him. Then he said 'Now hang on tight, I'm going to give you a bumpy ride.' And he crawled over to Ma. Whoopsie loved it.

When Ma saw them coming she laughed.

'Whoopsie's been growing up and you hadn't even noticed, had you, Pongo?' she said.

'No, I hadn't,' Pongo said. 'But how did she find me? I thought baby gorillas couldn't see very well.'

'Oh, Whoopsie can now,' Ma said. 'She watches you every day playing with your friends. She's dying to join you. In fact I was going to ask you, do you think she could play with you today?'

'She's too little,' Pongo said. 'She'll get knocked over and trodden on.'

'Not with her big brother to look after her,' Ma said.

'Oh, all right,' Pongo said. 'She can come on my back for the difficult bits.'

At playtime when Ma and Da lay down for a nap Pongo put Zambi at the front of a follow-my-leader and he came at the back carrying Whoopsie. At first they swung on creepers and Pongo found that Whoopsie could do that by herself. She had strong little arms and she could hang on. Then they did some running and jumping and for that Pongo carried Whoopsie on his back. When Zambi climbed a tree, Pongo began climbing it too with Whoopsie on his back. But Whoopsie had a surprise for him. She was much lighter than he was. She jumped off his back and ran up the tree ahead of him, much higher than he could go. But it was the first time she had ever climbed a tree and she got stuck.

'Go on without us,' Pongo called to the others. 'Whoopsie's stuck so I've got to rescue her.'

He had quite a job, too. The branches

were much too thin to take his weight so he couldn't climb up and fetch her. He had to get her down some other way.

'Now, Whoopsie, this game is called follow-my-leader and you have to follow me and I'm going down. Now come on,' Pongo called up to her.

Pongo put his arms round the trunk and slid down to the bottom. Whoopsie did not move. Ma was there watching and laughing.

'It's all right, Pongo,' she said. 'I'll fetch Whoopsie. I'm much lighter than you and I can get up there.'

But Da said, 'No, Ma, you stay here and we'll see if Pongo can get her down. He's no fool.'

'But she'll get frightened,' Ma said. 'I must go to her.'

'No,' Pongo said. 'Da is right. I know what he means. Whoopsie wants to feel that she's like the rest of us now and not a baby any more. If Ma fetches her she's still a baby and she won't like that.'

Da looked at Ma. 'Pongo's growing up, too,' he said. 'He's going to be a good brother for Whoopsie. Let's see what he'll do next.'

Pongo was already half way up the tree again. He got as high as he could and then he called up to Whoopsie.

'Come on, there's a place just behind you where you can put your foot. Look down and find it. I can see better than you from here and I'll tell you where to put your feet. You just hang on with your arms and do what I tell you. You're a big girl now, you can do it.'

'I'm frightened,' she said.

'Rubbish,' said Pongo. 'I'll catch you if you fall, but you won't. You're a good climber. Now, come on. Put your foot where I said.'

Whoopsie did that, and in a few minutes she was down as far as Pongo was.

'I did it,' she said. 'I did it.'

'I knew you could,' Pongo said. 'You're not a baby any more, are you? You're a big girl. Now this last bit you can't do because your arms aren't long enough to go right round the tree. So just put them round my neck and I'll take you down on my back.'

So they slid down like that together and

then Pongo ran after the others to catch
them up.

'Come on, Ma,' said Da. 'I think we can
leave Pongo to look after Whoopsie.'

'I can see that,' Ma said. 'I don't seem to
be needed round here any more.'

Da laughed. 'I don't think Pongo is going
to be able to give Whoopsie her milk,' he said.
'Now now or ever. So Whoopsie will need you
as much as I do.' And he put his arm round
her and led her away.

Ma looked up at Da. 'You're right,' she
said. 'But Pongo is a good brother. He'll
teach her a lot. And she's so pleased that now
she can play with the others. It's a shame
that there aren't any babies her own size for
her to play with.'

'Pongo understands that,' Da said.

'That's why he's helping. Look, there's a nice sunny spot over there. Let's have a nap.'

So they went to lie down while Pongo chased after the others with Whoopsie on his back.

Lessons

From then on, Whoopsie played with the other young gorillas every day, and poor Pongo became her teacher. He couldn't play with the others any more because he had to keep an eye on his little sister. Sometimes they played at fighting and Whoopsie was much too small. So when the bigger ones started to fight, Pongo found her a creeper to swing on. Whoopsie loved that.

The difficult thing was tree-climbing. Whoopsie couldn't forget the time she had got stuck. Pongo thought Whoopsie a good climber and wanted to get her climbing again. So one day he put her on his back and clambered up the first part of a tree.

'Now, Whoopsie,' he said, 'you go up the next bit on your own. I can't do that, but you can.'

'Yes,' Whoopsie said.

But what she climbed was his head. She stood on his shoulders and hung on to his ears.

'I've done it,' she said.

'You haven't done anything,' said Pongo.

'I have,' said Whoopsie, 'You said I was to climb up the next bit.'

'Of the tree, not me,' Pongo said.

But Whoopsie wasn't moving, so Pongo

slid down to the ground with Whoopsie still on his shoulders.

'I could climb down this tree, too,' Whoopsie said, climbing down his back and clutching handfuls of fur as she went.

Zambi was laughing at the bottom. 'Poor Pongo,' he said. 'So now you're a tree!'

'Very funny,' said Pongo. 'Now look here, Zambi, you must help me.'

So they hatched a plot. Next day, Pongo climbed another tree with Whoopsie on his back. He told her to go a little way up and come back to him.

'You know I can't do that,' she said.

Pongo grinned across at Zambi, who was up the next tree and had been told what to say.

'She can't do that,' Zambi said, 'she's only a baby.'

That was enough for Whoopsie. She quickly went up to where Pongo had pointed. Then, more slowly, she came back to him. Pongo looked at Zambi. 'There, she's no baby,' he said. 'I told you she was a good climber.'

There was no stopping Whoopsie now. Up and down she went like a yo-yo. Then she tried to climb down to the ground.

'This is the wrong sort of tree for you,' said Pongo. 'It's too wide for you to get your arms around. We'll find a better tree tomorrow that you can climb up and down.'

Pongo gave Whoopsie a tree-climbing lesson every day. Soon she could get higher than anyone else, because she was so small.

Running was another thing that Pongo had to teach his little sister. Whoopsie still crawled on her knees like a human baby.

'Straighten your legs at the back,' Pongo said, 'and curl your hands on the ground, so that you walk on your knuckles like I do. You can run much faster like that.'

Pongo had to work hard that day, because Whoopsie kept falling over when she ran after the others. He walked swiftly behind her at the back of the pack and picked her up when she fell. She soon learned to walk on her four feet.

'She learns very quickly,' said Pongo. 'You never have to tell her anything more than once.'

'Maybe,' said Zambi, 'but I find it very boring because there's nobody left for me to fight with.'

'Yes, there is,' said Pongo. 'Whoopsie's tired now, so I'll take her back to Ma.'

Then they had a good fight. It was true

that Pongo and Zambi could not play with the others in the way that they used to. They were both getting too big.

One day they were all playing follow-my-leader, a favourite game. In the middle of the game they crawled over Ma's tummy. She was used to this, and didn't mind at all. But Zambi was much too heavy, so he jumped over her. Pongo was a little way behind, looking after Whoopsie, as usual. She loved the idea of crawling all over Ma.

On the other side of Ma, Da was resting. the others would never climb over him, and had walked round his feet. But Whoopsie hadn't seen this. She climbed on to Da's tummy as well. It was round and bouncy, and she began to bounce up and down. Da just smiled.

Then she did a dreadful thing. She picked
up her fist and bashed Da's big shiny nose.
That hurt, and Da turned his head to one side.

When gorillas do that it means they are very cross, although Da was only doing it to protect his nose. But Whoopsie was horrified, and scampered back to Pongo.

'Da's cross with me,' she sobbed.

Pongo held out his arms and gave her a hug. Whoopsie was crying. 'Da's never been cross with me before,' she said.

'Well,' Pongo said. 'It hurts having your nose bashed. I don't think he's cross, he's just hurt. You bash your nose gently and you'll see.'

Whoopsie picked up her little fist and banged her nose hard.

'Oooh,' she howled. 'It does hurt.'

'You silly thing,' Pongo said. 'You didn't have to bang it as hard as that. But now you know why Da turned his head, don't you?'

'Yes,' Whoopsie sniffed.

'Well,' Pongo said, 'let's go and find a present for Da, to show you're sorry. Come on. I know what he'll like.'

A few minutes later Da felt a tug on his arm. There was Whoopsie with a piece of bamboo in her hand. 'It's a sorry present, Da,' she said. 'I didn't mean to hurt you.'

'I know,' Da said. 'this is a lovely piece of bamboo. Thank you, Whoopsie.'

'You're not cross any more?' Whoopsie said.

'Of course not,' Da said, and he put his arm round her. 'Now you go to Ma and have a nice drink of milk.'

And that's what Whoopsie did.

Sou'westers

A day or two later Whoopsie went running to her mother.

'Ma,' she said. 'The rain has pebbles in it.'

Ma laughed. 'It's hail,' she said. 'Little pieces of ice falling from the sky.'

'Ice?' Whoopsie said.

'Frozen water,' Ma said. 'Anyway, it's hard. And it hurts, doesn't it? We must get under the trees, I expect that's where Da will take us. Yes, look, there he is. He's beckoning to us.'

It was a heavy hailstorm. Gorillas hate getting wet and Da took them under some trees as quickly as he could. But poor little Whoopsie found that the pebbles were hurting her head.

'Come on,' Ma said. 'Get under my tummy.'

That's where Pongo and Zambi saw her: crouching under Ma's tummy.

'Poor little thing,' Pongo said. 'Her fur isn't as strong as ours yet.'

'Look,' Zambi said. 'The creeper's got a special covering on his head.'

The man was with them as usual and, of course, he was wearing a sou'wester. Pongo looked at him for a moment then he said to

Zambi, 'We must get something like that for Whoopsie. And for ourselves, come on.'

They went further into the forest and hunted for some head coverings. It was Zambi who found them. He picked one up and put it on his head. It was a plant with a sort of round crown of thick leaves with a flower in the middle.

'Oh, you do look pretty!' Pongo said when he saw him. 'But does it keep the hail off?'

'Yes,' Zambi said. 'I can't feel a thing. It's marvellous.'

Pongo picked one and put it on his head. 'You're right,' he said. 'Come on, let's pick some more for the others.'

They were soon back under the tree wearing their pretty hats. They had one for Whoopsie and one for Ma. Pongo put a hand

out to Whoopsie and drew her towards him. He
put the hat on her head while Ma put hers on.
Soon all the gorillas were wearing pretty hats.
Pongo and Zambi showed them where to find
them. Da laughed and laughed at his troop
but he got a pretty hat, too. Who cared about
hailstorms now? Whoopsie was still kneeling
under Ma's tummy because the hail hurt her
all over, but she had noticed something.

'Ma,' she said, tugging at her mother's arm.
'Everybody's standing up like the creeper.'

'Yes,' Ma said. 'We always stand up in
the rain. What do you think I'm doing? We
don't get so wet like this.'

'Well, I must, too, then,' said Whoopsie.

'No, you're too little to stand up yet,' said
Ma. 'You just stay where you are.'

But just then Pongo came past and

Whoopsie called to him, 'Teach me to stand up, Pongo.'

Zambi turned to Pongo and laughed. 'You have two new jobs,' he said. 'You seem to be more of a father than a brother to that baby.'

'No, just a teacher,' Pongo said. 'And you'll have to be one too today, because it'll need two of us to hold her up, one each side. Come on.'

So that's what they did. Whoopsie stood between them on her hind feet and they pulled

her along and taught her to walk. The hail
stopped and turned to rain, but Whoopsie still
went on with her walking lesson.

'Pull me faster,' she said suddenly. 'I
think I can run.'

She could too. Pongo and Zambi ran along beside her holding her hands. Gorillas hate rain but they forgot about it, they were so busy. Suddenly Whoopsie said, 'Take me to Da. I want to show Da I can run. I'm a big girl now.'

Pongo looked at Zambi. 'I wish she were a big bigger,' he said, 'My back feels as if it's coming in half.'

'So does mine,' said Zambi. 'But come on, let's take her to the Big Boss to show off, and perhaps she'll give up.'

When they got near to Da she said, 'Now let go, both of you.'

'You'll fall over,' Pongo said.

'No, I won't,' said Whoopsie. 'Now, let go.'

They did so and Whoopsie ran to Da with her hat over one ear. Da had been watching the walking and running lesson, but he pretended to be very surprised.

'Well, you are growing up,' he said, scooping her up. 'But now you must stop for a bit or you'll be worn out. I can see that poor Pongo and Zambi are.'

They were stretching and groaning with their pretty hats askew. Da put Whoopsie on Ma's back.

'I'm hungry,' she said.

'Come on, it's stopped raining, we'll go and find something to eat,' Ma said.

Which is exactly what they did.

Rescue

Zambi was complaining to Pongo. 'I don't think this is much of a job, being at the back of the troop,' he said. 'Nothing ever happens. I haven't needed to bang my chest or roar or anything yet.'

'I know,' Pongo said. 'But I suppose we should be glad that nothing dangerous ever happens.'

He'd spoken too soon. Something

dangerous did happen. There wasn't a leopard or a man with a gun, but Pongo's little sister was up to her tricks again. They were coming along a path by a stream. gorillas are afraid of water so they don't go near it, but Whoopsie didn't know that and she had found a fallen tree across the stream. Ma had only taken her eyes off her for a moment but it was enough. Pongo at the back of the troop suddenly heard a cry from the middle of the stream.

'Look at me.'

'There was Whoopsie on a branch bouncing up and down. Pongo beat his chest and roared. Ma and Da had to know about this. Da came rushing back and Pongo pointed at Whoopsie.

'Oh, my goodness,' Da said. 'Come back, Whoopsie. Come back.'

Whoopsie liked it in the middle of the stream so she pretended not to understand what Da was saying. 'I'll have to fetch her,' Da said.

'No,' said Ma. 'You're much too heavy for that little tree.'

'I'll fetch her,' Pongo said. 'I'm much lighter than Da. I can get across the stream further up and chase Whoopsie back. She'll come if I make a game of it.'

Pongo hurried along the path. He was quite right, it was narrower further up and there were stepping stones. It wasn't very deep either. He went carefully across the stepping stones and then ran along the bank to the other end of the tree Whoopsie was on. It was a bit thin this end and he was afraid it might not take his weight, but he crawled along very carefully and when he was quite sure that he could balance he called out to Whoopsie, 'I'm coming for you.'

Whoopsie turned round. 'Pongo,' she said. 'How did you get over there? Are you coming to play with me. Come and see what I've found. There are some funny things going under the tree, they're going very fast; silvery things.'

'Fish,' Pongo said. 'And I can go very fast, too, and I'm coming after you. I'm a big fish and I'm going to gobble you up.'

And he began to crawl as fast as he could across the tree.

'You can't catch me,' Whoopsie said. She liked chasing games. She began to crawl as fast as she could towards the bank.

'I hope she won't come too fast and fall in,' Ma said.

'I don't think she will,' said Da. 'She has more sense than she seems to have. Anyway, Pongo's there. He'll fish her out if he has to.'

The chase went on. Pongo crawled as fast as he could while Whoopsie crawled and looked round and crawled and looked round to get away from Pongo.

All the gorillas were standing along
the bank watching.

Pongo's game worked. In a few minutes
Whoopsie was near the bank. Da reached out
his great hand and grabbed her.

'Put me down,' Whoopsie yelled. 'Pongo will catch me.'

'Yes, do put her down,' Ma said. 'This is a chasing game. Pongo knows what he's doing.'

So Da let Whoopsie run away and climb a creeper while Pongo crawled the last bit across the tree. He grinned at Da.

'Panic over,' he said. 'But oh, that sister of mine. She's more trouble than all the rest of you put together.'

'You're telling me,' said Da. 'But thank you, Pongo, that tree would never have taken my weight.'

Pongo saw that Da was a bit disappointed that he hadn't been able to do it himself. So he said, 'Da, let's move the tree so she can't do it again. I can't lift it but I expect you can.'

Da went to the tree and with one big

heave moved it sideways. Then with a second heave he threw it out into the stream.

'Oh, good,' said Ma, 'Now she won't be able to reach it.'

'I'd better go on with the chase, I suppose,' Pongo said. 'Let's hope the creeper will take the weight of both of us.'

But he didn't have to bother because Whoopsie had seen what her father had done.

'Da, what have you done with my tree? You've thrown it away.'

'Yes,' Da said. 'I like throwing trees about. It gives me an appetite for breakfast. Come on. We'll go and find some.'

And he put Whoopsie on Ma's back and went on in front of the troop. Pongo was waiting to come along at the back with Zambi.

'My feet are wet,' he complained to Zambi.

'I hate wet feet.'

Zambi laughed. 'Well, you shouldn't go paddling before breakfast,' he said.

'It was those stepping stones, said Pongo.

'Oh well,' said Zambi. 'You're a brother and brothers have to get used to wet feet.'

'Not this one,' Pongo said. 'I shan't rescue her again.'

But of course he didn't mean it and Zambi knew that. A bit later on when they were eating Da came up to Pongo.

'I want to thank you, Pongo,' he said. 'I don't know what I'd do without you.'

'Well, I don't know what we'd do without you,' Pongo said. 'I can't throw trees about like that. Whoopsie would have been in the middle of the stream again by now if you hadn't moved it. She is a little monkey!'

Da laughed and laughed. 'You're quite right there, son,' he said. 'Quite right.'

The hunter

A few days later they were back in the part
of the forest they remembered well. They
were eating when Zambi came up to Pongo.
'I saw the creeper go,' he said. 'He's left
the troop.'

Pongo laughed. 'No,' he said, 'he's
probably just gone back to his nest. You
know, that wooden one. He lives near here.'

'Oh, yes,' Zambi said, and he was soon

back eating again.

They were just going off to play when Ma came rushing towards them.

'Have you seen Whoopsie?' she said. 'I can't find her anywhere.'

They looked for her for a while and then Pongo said to Zambi, 'I bet I know where she is. You know how nosey she is now. She might have followed the man to see where he was going.'

'Oh, yes,' Zambi said. 'You're probably right.'

'We'll go and tell Ma and Da where we're going,' said Pzongo. 'We'll have to go and fetch her. It's quite a long way, though; I don't expect she's all the way there yet.'

'We'll go on ahead, Zambi and I,' Pongo said to Ma and Da, so they began to hurry through the forest towards the clearing where the man's nest was. They found Whoopsie up a tree.

'Pongo,' she called. 'Look, there's another man now.'

Pongo looked. Whoopsie was right. There was a new box on wheels and there were two men coming out of the nest, the creeper with his white head and a smaller man, but big, like Da. But Pongo saw something else. The second man had a gun on his arm.

'Quick,' he said to Zambi. 'Go and tell Da. I'll get Whoopsie.'

Zambi began to argue. 'Da's coming,' he said.

'Do what you're told,' said Pongo. 'We may need Da. You know what guns can do.'

Zambi went off. But the damage was done.

Whoopsie had climbed down the tree and run towards the men. She didn't know about guns. Pongo didn't know what to do for a second. Should he beat his chest and roar? But then he heard Ma and Da behind him. So he ran straight out after Whoopsie. It was all over in a moment. There was a loud bang. Pongo threw himself on top of Whoopsie. He looked up to see that their man had knocked the gun out of the hunter's hands onto the ground. Ma and Da had reached the edge of the forest and had seen it too and they saw the hunter leap onto their man who was lying on the gun.

'Take them back,' Da said to Ma. 'That old man can't do much more.'

And then he charged with an enormous roar. The hunter looked up and saw the great ape coming at him. He couldn't reach the gun. He just turned and ran towards the box on wheels. The Big Boss chased him and took a big bite out of the seat of his trousers. The hunter yelled as he got into his car and drove away with a screech of tyres. The Big Boss turned round. Their man was limping slowly back into his nest carrying the hunter's gun.

Da wanted to thank him but he didn't know how to. What that man needs is a rest, he thought, and I'll leave him to it. He went back towards the forest. Pongo ran to meet him.

'Da,' he said. 'You attacked that hunter. You told me that gorillas never attack man.'

'They do if men attack their young,' Da said. 'He was trying to shoot you. Anyway,

that bite won't kill him, it will only hurt him. But he'll be back with some friends. We must get up into the mountains quickly.'

'But what about the creeper?' said Pongo. 'He saved my life. I ought to thank him.'

'That old man just needs a good sleep,' said Da. 'He's feeling his age like me and there's no point in him saving your life if you stay down here and lost it. Now come on. We'll catch up the others, and have a rest and some food. Then we'll start up into the mountains.'

On the way back Pongo said to Da, 'Whoopsie shouldn't have run out like that, should she? She has a lot to learn.'

'Well,' Da said, 'the only man she has met is the creeper who is a nice man. She didn't know about the other kind. I think she was frightened by the bang. She'll have to learn like you that there are nice men and nasty men. And you have to find out which they are before you go near them.'

When they reached the others Whoopsie was having milk from Ma because it made her feel better. 'She was very frightened,' Ma said.

'Good,' said Da. 'Now she'll be much safer. She won't always have a nice man like the creeper around to save her. Or Pongo.'

'Yes, she will,' Pongo said. 'I'll stay with the troop, Da.'

Ma looked at Da, who couldn't speak.

'I told you he would,' she said. 'Pongo knows he's needed.'

Later on when Pongo and Zambi were coming up at the back of the troop Zambi said to Pongo, 'Did you see the Big Boss when he charged? He had all his hair standing on end and he looked twice as big as he is.'

'Yes,' Pongo said. 'It was to frighten the hunter.'

'I noticed something else, too,' Zambi said. 'The Big Boss is turning silver all over. It's not just his back now. His chest and everything's silver.'

'Of course it is,' said Pongo. 'He's not getting any younger. That's why he needs us. that's something I wanted to ask you about, Zambi. I'm going to stay with the troop to help Da because he's getting older. Will you stay too and help me?'

'Yes,' Zambi said. 'I don't want to go and start a troop of my own. I want to stay with you and my friends here.'

'Good!' Pongo said.

A bit later on Da pulled up and they all

settled down to eat. Whoopsie stayed very close to Ma at this time. She wasn't likely to go wandering off by herself for a long time. Before they settled down for the night Da said, 'Now we're going to go to bed early. Sleep well, because we're going a long way up into the mountains tomorrow, where we'll be quite safe from men with guns. They don't go up there.'

So they bedded down and slept soundly.

Up

They kept climbing all the next day, stopping to eat and sleep and play as usual, but on the second day they found themselves at the foot of a very bare rocky bit of mountain. Da called them all together. 'Now,' he said. 'We're all going to climb up here. It's quite flat and safe at the top and there's plenty of food but this bit will be hard for some of you. But I've never seen a man up there.'

'Not even a good one,' Whoopsie said.

'No, I haven't seen any sort of man, good or bad, who can climb up this. But we can. Now, I want everyone to go up in the front except Zambi and Pongo and me. We'll stay at the back to help anyone who gets stuck. Just yell and one of us will come over and help you. The main thing is use your eyes. See where you can put your hands and feet. Now, off you go. Just call for help if you get frightened or stuck. We won't be far behind.'

'It is difficult,' Zambi said to Pongo as they started to climb. 'The rock's so slippery.'

'I suppose that's what keeps the men away,' Pongo said. 'That's why Da's brought us here. He knows what he's doing.'

It was strange. The youngsters found it easier than the older ones because they were lighter and more nimble and they hadn't got the weight to lift. But, of course, Whoopsie, who was still only a baby, got stuck two or three times. Every time she called, Da went to help her. But the third time he gave her a lecture.

'Now, Whoopsie,' he said. 'It's not clever to find the hardest way up. Look for the easiest way.'

'I didn't know it was going to be hard,' she said.

'No, of course you didn't,' Da said. 'You've never climbed a mountain like this before. You're the youngest. But this is a good mountain. Put your feet on my shoulders and reach up and you'll be able to get free.'

'I'm frightened,' she said.

'You've no need to be frightened when I'm here,' Da said. 'Hang on to my head, put your feet on my shoulders and then pull yourself up. 'It's quite easy the next bit of the way. And I'll catch you if you fall. But you won't.'

Whoopsie was soon safe.

'Stay near Ma from now on,' Da said. 'She knows what she's doing. I don't want to see you stuck again.'

Whoopsie was learning. She didn't get stuck again. But – oh dear! – the Big Boss was stuck. He had been so busy helping Whoopsie that he hadn't noticed that there were no hand-holds for him. He had to call Pongo.

'The old buffer's stuck!' Da said.

Pongo grinned. 'Not for long,' he said. 'Pongo's coming to help. Though how he's going to I don't know. You can't stand on my shoulders; I can't take your weight. I know,

I'll climb up and see if that tree is strong enough for me to hang on to.'

He climbed up and it was firm and strong. He looked over the edge of the cliff to Da.

'Now,' he said. 'I'm going to wrap my arms round the tree and make myself into a creeper, and you're to climb up using my legs like a creeper.'

'Are you sure?' asked Da.

'Of course I'm sure,' said Pongo, which was a bit of a whopper, but it was the only way he could think of to help Da. 'Now I'll yell when I've got my arms round the tree,' Pongo said. 'All right?'

'All right,' Da said.

So Pongo wrapped himself round the tree as firmly as he could.

'Come on,' he said.

Da pulled himself up as Pongo had told him, taking as much weight as he could on one arm and hanging onto Pongo with the other. He got free.

'Thank you, Pongo,' Da said when he reached him.

Pongo unwrapped his arms from the tree.

'How are you feeling?' asked Da.

'I think I've been pulled in half,' Pongo said.

But he stood up and he was quite all right. They climbed the rest of the way together.

Da said to Pongo, 'I'm getting too old for this lark, I think you'll have to be the leader of the troop now.'

'No,' Pongo said, 'I'm much too young.

I don't look like the leader of the troop. You'll have to wait until I've got a silver back and look like a leader. And I don't know as much as you do, so you'll have to wait until I know as much as a leader. You've got lots to teach me. Will you do that, Da?'

'Yes, son, but I'm getting old. I've never got stuck on a mountain before.'

'All right,' Pongo said. 'You're too old and I'm too young, but we can work together. Zambi will help, too. I've talked to him about it, and he wants to stay with the troop.'

'Well, when you've got a silver back you can be the leader of the troop – the Big Boss. And I'll go at the back with Zambi.'

'That won't be for a long time yet,' Pongo said.

They soon found some forest at the top

of the mountain which had plenty of food and they were happy there for a long time. One day Da had a lovely surprise. Whoopsie came running to him.

'Da,' she said. 'I've been riding on Pongo's back and he's got three white hairs like you. That means he's growing up, doesn't it?'

'Yes,' Da said. 'It does, and that means all our troubles will soon be over!'

This is Hilda.

Hilda is a small, speckled hen.
She is brave and very determined.
And when Hilda makes up her mind,
nothing and no one can stop her!

Read all about Hilda's adventures in
The Hen Who Wouldn't Give Up

This is Pat.

Pat is a little sea otter
as curious as can be.

She loves turning up her toes
and floating in the sea!

Read all about Pat's adventures in
The Otter Who Wanted to Know

This is Suzy.

High in a hot air balloon,
flying away, all alone.

How is Suzy the cat ever
going to find her way home?

Read all about Suzy's adventures in
The Cat Who Wanted to Go Home

This is Otto.

Otto is a penguin chick.
He likes to play in the snow.
But first he'll teach the other
chicks all they need to know.

Read all about Otto's adventures in
The Penguin Who Wanted to Find Out